Richard Henry Major

The Bibliography of the First Letter of Christopher Columbus

His Discovery of the New World

Richard Henry Major

The Bibliography of the First Letter of Christopher Columbus
His Discovery of the New World

ISBN/EAN: 9783744727846

Printed in Europe, USA, Canada, Australia, Japan

THE BIBLIOGRAPHY

OF THE

FIRST LETTER

OF

CHRISTOPHER COLUMBUS,

DESCRIBING

HIS DISCOVERY OF THE NEW WORLD.

BY

R. H. MAJOR, F.S.A., &c.

Keeper of the Department of Maps and Charts in the British Museum, and
Hon. Sec. of the Royal Geographical Society.

LONDON:
ELLIS & WHITE, 29 NEW BOND STREET.
1872.

LONDON:
Printed by JOHN STRANGEWAYS, Castle St. Leicester Sq.

BIBLIOGRAPHY,

&c.

In this bibliographical notice I do not propose to deal with any editions of the first letter of Columbus beyond the 'Incunabula,' which I arrange in the order of their publication, as ascertained from an examination of the documents themselves.

1. ¶ Epistola Christofori Colom : cui etas nostra multũ debet : de | Insulis Indie supra Gangem nuper inuẽtis. Ad quas perqren- | das octauo antea mense auspiciis & ere inuictissemor' Fernãdi & | Helisabet Hispaniar' Regũ missus fuerat : ad magnificum dñm | Gabrielem Sanchis eorundẽ serenissimor' Regum Tesaurariũ | missa : quã nobilis ac litteratus vir Leander de Cosco ab Hispa | no idiomate in latinum cõuertit tertio kal's Maii M.cccc.xciii | Pontificatus Alexandri Sexti Anno primo.

B

Small 4to. This edition, which, as I shall presently show, is the *editio princeps*, was printed by Stephen Plannck at Rome in 1493. It consists of four leaves, printed in gothic type, and has 33 lines in a full page. Copies are in the Grenville and King's Libraries in the British Museum.

2. ¶ Epistola Christofori Colom : cui etas nostra multum debet : de | Insulis Indie super Gangem nuper inuētis. Ad quas perquiren | das octauo antea mense auspiciis & ere inuictissimorum Fernandi | ac Helisabet Hispaniar' Regū missus fuerat : ad Magnificū dūm | Gabrielem Sanches : eorundem serenissimorum Regum Tesau | rariū missa : Quā generosus ac litteratus vir Leander de Cosco ab | Hispano idiomate in latinū cōuertit : tertio Kalen' Maij M.cccc. | xc.iij. Pontificatus Alexandri Sexti Anno Primo.

End :—

¶ Impressit Rome Eucharius Argenteus [Silber] Anno dūi. M.ccccxciij.

Small 4to. three leaves, printed in

gothic letter; 40 lines in a page. A copy is in the Grenville Library.

3. ℂ Epistola Christofori Colom: cui etas nostra multū debet: de | Insulis Indię supra Gangem nuper inuentis. Ad quas perqui | rendas octauo antea mense auspicijs & ere invictissimi Fernan | di Hispaniarum Regis missus fuerat: ad Magnificum dñm Ra | phaelem Sanxis: eiusdem serenissimi Regis Tesaurariū missa: | quam nobilis ac litteratus vir Aliander de Cosco ab Hispano | ideomate in latinum conuertit: tertio kal's Maij. M.cccc.xciij. | Pontificatus Alexandri Sexti Anno Primo.

Small 4to. Gothic letter; four leaves, 34 lines in a full page. This edition is supposed to have been printed by Stephen Plannck at Rome, about 1493. 3 or 4 copies are known; two are in the General Library and Grenville Library, British Museum.

4. De Insulis inuentis | Epistola Cristoferi Colom (cui etas nostra | multū debet): de Insulis in mari Indico nup' | inuētis. Ad

quas perquirendas octauo antea | mense : auspicijs et ere Invictissimi Fernandi | Hispaniarum Regis missus fuerat) ad Mag | nificum dñm Raphaelez Sanxis : eiusdē sere | nissimi Regis Thesaurariū missa. quam nobi | lis ac litterat' vir Aliander d'Cosco : ab His | pano ydeomate in latinū conuertit : tercio k'ls | Maij. M.cccc.xciij. Pontificatus Alexandri | Sexti Anno Primo.

Small 8vo. Gothic character; ten leaves, 26 and 27 lines in a page. The title above given is preceded by a leaf bearing on the recto the arms of Spain, 'Regnū hyspanie'—on the verso the cut of the 'Oceanica Classis.' There are 6 woodcuts—the 'Oceanica Classis' being repeated. A copy is in the Grenville Library.

5. Epistola de insulis de | nouo repertis. Impressa | parisius in cāpo gaillardi.

Small 4to. Gothic letter; four leaves, 39 lines in a full page. This edition was printed by Guy Marchand about 1494.

Brunet states that the only copy known is that formerly belonging to M. Ternaux-Compans, now the property of Mr. John Carter Brown; but there is another copy in the Bibliothèque Impériale, as will be seen by the title of the reprint, as follows:—'Lettre de Christophe Colomb sur la découverte du Nouveau-Monde, publiée d'après la rarissime version latine conservée à la Bibliothèque Impériale. Traduite en Français, commentée et enrichie de notes puisées aux sources originales par Lucien de Rosny.' 8vo., Paris, 1865.

6. Epistola de insulis noui | ter repertis Impressa parisius In campo gaillardi.

Small 4to. Gothic letter; four leaves, 39 lines in a page. The above title is in two lines, the first printed in a larger character. Underneath is the device of the printer, 'Guiot Marchant'—two cobblers at work, one cutting the leather, the other making it up. This edition was printed by Guy Marchand at Paris, about 1494.

A copy is in the Bodleian Library. A facsimile made by Mr. John Harris, sen., is in the British Museum; the impression was limited to five copies.

All the foregoing editions have at the end the Latin Epigram in eight verses of R. L. de Corbatia (a pseudonym for Leonardus de Carninis, Bishop of Monte Peloso in Naples). In this edition, below the epigram, on the same page, is a woodcut of the Angel appearing to the Shepherds. Mr. Lenox has given a facsimile of this in the Appendix to *Syllacius*. The title on the recto of the following leaf (sig. a, ij) is the same as in the Roman editions, having the name of Ferdinand, without that of Isabella. It ends with the words: 'Vale. Ulisbone pridie Idus Marcij.'

A 'pictorial' edition of the Latin letter, in 4to., was printed in 1494. It is appended to a work by Carolus Verardus, 'In laudem Serenissimi Ferdinandi Hispaniar' regis. . . . Et de Insulis in mari Indico nuper inuentis.'

The work is printed on fifteen pages in Roman characters, and probably at Basle, by B. de Olpe. The woodcuts are the same as those used in the small 8vo. edition printed about 1493 (see No. 4).

No sooner did this letter make its appearance in print in the year 1493, than the narrative it contained was put forth in Italian *ottava rima* by Giuliano Dati, one of the most popular poets of the day; and there is reason to believe that it was sung about the streets to announce to the Italians the astounding news of the discovery of a new world.

The copy of this curious and valuable poem, reprinted in my first edition of the 'Select Letters of Columbus,' in 1847, was at that time believed to be unique.

¶ La lettera dellisole che ha trouato nuovamente il Re dispagna.

End: —

¶ Finita lastoria della iuẽtione del | le nuoue isole dicãnaria ĩdiane trac | te duna pistola dixpofano colõbo & | ꝑmesser Giuliano dati tradocta di la | tino ĩ uersi uulgari allaude della ce | lestiale corte & aconsolatione della | christiana religione & apghiera del magnifico caualiere messer Giouã | filippo del ignamine domestico fa | miliare dello illustrissimo Re dispa | gna xpĩanissimo a di. xxvi. docto | bre. 14.93. Florentie.

4to. Printed in Roman characters on four leaves, in double columns. The poem consists of 68 stanzas in *ottava rima.*

Beneath the single-line title is a woodcut representing the landing of Columbus, and King Ferdinand seated on his throne on the *opposite shore.* This is the only copy known.

Since 1847 another edition has been acquired by the British Museum, bearing the following title:—

> ¶ Questa e la hystoria della inuentiõe delle diese Isole di Cannaria In | diane extracte duna Epistola di Christofano Colombo & per messer Giu | liano Dati traducta de latino in uersi uulgari a laude e gloria della cele | stiale corte & a consolatione della christiana religiõe & apreghiera del ma | gnifico Caualier miser Giouanfilippo Delignamine domestico familia | re dello Sacratissimo Re di spagna Christianissimo a di. xxv. doctobre. | M.cccclxxxxiii.
>
> End:—
>
> FINIS
>
> Joannes dictus Florentinus.

4to. Printed in gothic characters, in double columns, and, without doubt, at Florence. A complete copy should contain four leaves. The copy in the British Museum, the only one of this edition hitherto discovered, is, unfortunately, deficient in two leaves—viz., the second and the third. It is printed in a very rude type on coarse paper, and was evidently a popular edition, sold at a very small price. This edition presents many variations from the other, both in the orthography and language, and omits the final stanza, which is little else than the colophon of the other versified :—

Questa ha cõposta de' dati Giuliano
etc. etc. etc.

¶ Eyn schön hübsch lesen von etlichen insslen | die do in kurtzen zyten funden synd durch dẽ | künig von hispania. vnd sagt võ grossen wun | derlichen dingen die in dẽ selbẽ insslen synd.

End :—

Getruckt zũ strassburg vff gruneck võ meister Bartlomess | küstler ym iar. M.cccc.xcvij. vff sant Jeronymus tag.

Small 4to. Seven leaves, 30 lines in a page. Beneath the title is a woodcut representing the apprehension of Christ in the garden; this is repeated on the verso of the last leaf. This edition is very rare. A copy is in the Grenville Library.

Besides the foregoing we are in possession of a photo-zincographic facsimile published at Milan in 1866, by the Marquis Gerolamo d'Adda, of an early printed edition of the Spanish original, in the Ambrosian Library in that city. It bears no printer's name or place or date of publication, but it is unquestionably of the fifteenth century, and is considered by bibliographers to be of the date of 1493. Señor Pascual de Gayangos (in a valuable paper, entitled 'La Carta de Cristóbal Colon al Escribano Luis de Santangel,' printed in the Madrid Journal, *La America*, under date of 13th

April, 1867) suggests that it was printed in Lisbon.

We have also in Navarrete's *Coleccion de Viages*, printed at Madrid 1825, vol. i. pp. 167–175, what professes to be an attested literal rendering of a copy of Columbus's letter in Spanish to the Escribano de Racion (whom we know from Argensola's *Anales de Aragon* to be Luis de Santangel), in the Archives at Simancas.

And, further, we have a printed version of a copy of the first letter in Spanish MS., discovered by His Excellency Senhor de Varnhagen in Valencia, and published by him in that city in 1858, under the title of *Primera Epistola del Almirante Don Christóbal Colon .... a D. Gabriel Sanchez Tesorero de Aragon*. As editor, Senhor de Varnhagen assumed the pseudonym of D.

Genaro H. de Volafan; and last year His Excellency published at Vienna a little work, the nature and contents of which are explained by its title, which is as follows:—'Carta de Cristóbal Colon enviada de Lisboa a Barcelona en Marzo de 1493. Nueva Edicion Critica: Conteniendo las variantes de los diferentes textos, juicio sobre estos, reflexiones tendentes a mostrar a quien la Carta fue escrita, y varias otras noticias, por el Seudónimo de Valencia.'

Be it observed that in all these the *titles* are supplied by the respective editors, and consequently have no authority beyond the weight of each editor's individual opinion. I have carefully collated the three documents, and the result is a certain conclusion that neither one nor the other is a correct transcript of the original letter. The grounds for this conclusion are, that while no two of them entirely agree *inter se*, every one of them exhibits certain special errors which, as I shall presently demonstrate, *could* not have been in the original. The apparent rashness of this assertion will disappear if the reader will accompany me in my effort to detect which of the printed Latin editions which we possess is to receive the distinction of *editio princeps*. Various have been the opinions on this subject. Both Mr. Lenox and Brunet have given the lead to the edition which I have ventured to place *fourth*. Mr. Harrisse, in his elaborate *Notes on Columbus*, gives the first place to that which stands *third* in my series, and His Excellency Senhor de Varnhagen assigns priority to the edition which I make to be the *second*. That to which I assign the distinction of taking the lead has the *second* place given to it by Senhor de Varnhagen, and the *third* by Brunet, Mr. Lenox, and Harrisse. In offering a conclusion so much at variance with my predecessors, my only means of escaping the charge of presumption (but that I hope is an effectual one), is neither to adopt the opinion of any one else nor to offer any opinion of my own, but to reduce the matter to demonstration by facts either within or connected with the documents themselves.

On examination of the titles it will be seen that the six editions resolve themselves by several very strongly marked features into two distinct groups. One of these groups, embracing four of the editions, is characterized by remarkable inaccuracy in three separate points—all four exhibiting all these inaccuracies in common; while the remaining two, being free from them, stand clearly defined into a distinct group by themselves.

Thus; the titles of the editions numbered 3, 4, 5, 6, all speak of Columbus being sent out under the auspices and at the expense of Ferdinand, King of Spain, without reference to the name of Queen Isabella. They all describe the letter as addressed to the Treasurer 'Sanxis,' instead of 'Sanchez,' whose Christian name they pervert from 'Gabriel' to 'Raphael.' Furthermore, they all convert the Christian name of the translator from 'Leander' to 'Aliander.'

The titles of the editions numbered 1 and 2, on the contrary, give the names of both the sovereigns, call the Treasurer in No. 2 Sanches, in No. 1 'Sanchis,' but not Sanxis, and rightly name the translator 'Leander de Cosco.'

Now there is no difficulty in showing

which of these groups has the merit of correctness, or which the demerit of incorrectness.

It is perfectly well known that in 1493 Ferdinand and Isabella held the common title of *Reyes de España.* Whether 'Sanches' or 'Sanxis' should be the correct form of spelling the name of a Spaniard who was treasurer to the Spanish sovereigns, it would be waste of time to question, and that his Christian name was Gabriel and not Raphael, we have clear evidence from an independent document in the Archives of Simancas, dated December 1495, for which the reader is referred to Navarrete's *Coleccion de Viages*, vol. iii. p. 76, line 16, where he is called 'El tesorero Gabriel Sanchez.' His name is also mentioned more than once by Zurita in his *Anales de Aragon.*

The question then arises whether the palm of priority is to be conceded to the correct or to the incorrect form. Now all these six titles agree in stating that the original Spanish letter of Columbus was *sent* to the Treasurer Royal. But for a letter to be sent, it must carry an address, and if Columbus inserted in such address the Treasurer's name, he, who knew Spanish so well, would not have insulted that dignitary by converting his surname of Sanchez into Sanxis, or his Christian name of Gabriel into Raphael. But even if we suppose that he omitted the name altogether, as is probable, and simply superscribed his letter with the title of the Treasurer, the fact still remains that the translator or editor of the first edition derived the information that the letter was so sent, directly from the Treasurer himself, who at least knew his own name and would not allow it to be transmitted for publication (if Columbus had been guilty of the blunder) under the form of 'Raphael Sanxis.' Nor would he, holding a high official post, have been guilty of the *maladresse* of omitting the name of the Queen in the description of his own title. Now of our two groups of printed letters it is indisputable that that one must take precedence which comes immediately in connection with the original source, and as that source is at the same time the head-quarters of correctness, it follows that correctness must be the criterion of priority.

We thus find our six candidates for the glory of 'editio princeps' reduced to two. Now these two issued from two different printing-presses. One of them is printed by Argenteus, *i.e.* Silber, and bears his name with the imprint, 'Rome, 1493.' The other is without printer's name or place or date of publication, but is indisputably from the printing-press of Stephanus Plannck, as may be seen by comparing it with a work of Benedictus de Nursia of the same date, entitled, '*Incipit libellus de conservatione sanitatis secundum ordinem alphabeti distinctus per eximium doctorem magistrum Benedictum compositus.*' *Impressum Rome per magistrum Stephanum Planck. Anno Domini mccccxciii, quarto nōn Maii.* In this and other works from the same press the form and type precisely correspond with those of our letter.

Now these two editions of Plannck and Silber were either printed simultaneously or not. Instances of the same work being printed by two different printers on the same day do occur. One example is before me of this happening in this very year 1493. The work is entitled, '*Illustris et Reverendi Domini Nicolai Mariæ Estensis Episcopi Hadriensis oratio pro consanguineo suo inclyto Hercule Estensi Ferrariæ duce secundo.*' One edition, in Roman character, bears the colophon, *Romæ impressa per mgrm Planuck: Julio Campello Spoletino procurante. Anno Salvatoris mccccxxxxiii. Nonis Januariis.* The other, in Gothic character, bears precisely the same title and the same colophon, with the difference of the words, *impressa per magistrum Andream Fritag.* Both are small 4to, of the size of our two editions of the letter of Columbus.

But here it must be observed that there was apparently a special object in resorting to this exceptional procedure, viz., the production simultaneously of one edition in Roman and another in Gothic types, to suit the tastes of purchasers. In the case before us, however, the question of this motive does not arise, for both Plannck's and Silber's editions are in Gothic type; and any way it is clear that, in a case of the kind, the same text would be handed to each printer to set up, as any patent discrepancies between the two would be to the self-stultification of the editor. Now, in the case of the Columbus letter, such patent discrepancies do occur; by which I mean no mere printer's blunders, but deliberate alterations of Latin expressions, as for example, 'ambularunt' in Plannck is 'ambulaverunt' in Silber; 'serenissimos Reges nostros,' correct Latin in Plannck, is 'serenissimorum regum nostrorum,' making bad grammar, in Silber. This fact of itself I contend disproves simultaneity of production. But side by side with these discrepancies, we observe the repetition in the one of eccentricities or inaccuracies occurring in the other, as in the words 'quom,' 'benivolentia,' and 'nanque.' The former, though not incorrect, is quaint and unusual, but the two latter are faulty peculiarities, and their occurrence, in both editions, side by side with deliberate alterations, proves the one to be copied from the other either by the hand of the transcriber or of the compositor. This fact once established, I have to call attention to the following remarkable difference between the two editions. In the Planck edition the distance sailed by Columbus along the north coast of Hispaniola is stated as DLXIIII miles. In Silber's the same figures occur minus the D, and with no space left for the letter to have fallen out. Now it being understood that one of these is a copy from the other, whether through a transcriber's or a compositor's hand, if we suppose that the Silber edition, which was *minus* the D, appeared first, we must perceive that the error is one which no special knowledge could enable the editor or printer of the other to suspect, much less to rectify, and yet in the Planck edition we should find it so rectified. Whereas if the Planck edition be supposed to be the first, we have no such difficulty to encounter, but simply meet (in the Silber edition) with a negligent omission of a letter, which may so easily happen. The next enquiry, of course, is, which number is right, 564 or 64 miles? Fortunately we have the means of answering this question with certainty, for as we possess two copies, or copies of copies, of the original Spanish letter, we find that the translator, Leander de Cosco, converted the leagues of the Spanish original into miles by multiplying them, though ignorantly, by 3; and in one of these two copies, which can in other respects be shown to be far more correct than its fellow, these leagues are stated as 188, which correspond exactly with 564 miles. It must be clear, then, that the edition containing the number 564 was derived from the original accounts, while that which contained the number 64 had allowed the D to be lost. The result I submit to be that Plannck's edition must claim the palm to priority.

To this conclusion it has been objected by a friend that the argument is not complete, inasmuch as Cosco the translator may have sent his translation to

Rome, with instructions that a copy thereof should be made, and that, as the work was of importance, two printers should at once be employed in printing from the two copies; that the copyist may have thought fit to make the alterations which appear between the two, or, failing him, that these alterations may have been made by the compositor of one of them. To which I reply that the deviations in the Silber edition are all on the side of ignorance, and not such as could have been made by an original translator. To take the most notable example: in Planck's edition occurs this passage, already slightly referred to, 'quæ res perutilis est ad id quod Serenissimos Reges nostros exoptare præcipue reor,' 'Which thing is very useful for the object which I think that our most serene Sovereigns principally desire.' Here we find the right grammatical construction of the accusative before the infinitive mood, just as the translator would write it. In Silber's edition the sentence stands thus: 'quæ res perutilis est ad id quod Serenissimorum regum nostrorum exoptare præcipue reor,' a change showing such ignorance of grammatical construction that it could not have been the work of the translator. I contend that, under such circumstances, even if it should be assumed (though there is no warranty for such assumption) that the two editions were printed simultaneously, Planck's edition would justly take the lead on account of its more immediate derivation from the original translation.

But before I leave this subject I must call attention to a notable fact, which opens up the question whether the real *editio princeps* has perished, or not as yet come to our knowledge. It happens that the length of the north coast of Hispaniola is *twice* stated by Columbus in this letter. The *first* mention of it is given correctly in Planck's edition as 'milliaria dlxiiii,' which I have already shown to be a right number, while in Silber the 'd' is lost, and the number stands 'lxiiii.' The *second* mention of the length of the coast is given *alike incorrectly by both* as dxl. This fact, brought into combination with those evolved by our comparison of the two texts, not only corroborates the non-originality and secondary position of Silber's edition, but it raises a question as to whether Planck's was not preceded by another which has never come to our knowledge, in which both numbers were correctly given. It might be conjectured that Columbus himself wrote the second number incorrectly, but here the different Spanish texts come valuably to our aid, and the curious circumstance that the translator Cosco converted the leagues of the Spanish into miles in the Latin, supplies a most welcome means of solving the riddle. Another document, the contemporaneous rhythmical version of the letter by Giuliano Dati, will also be of great service in the examination of the subject. For the sake of clearness I will tabulate them, and distinguish the correct numbers, where they occur, by italics :—

	Ambrosian Text.	Valencia MS.	Simancas MS.	Planck's Edition.	Silber's Edition.	Dati.
First ention	clxxviii leguas.	*ciento e ochenta y ocho leguas.*	ciento e setenta y ocho leguas.	milliaria *dlxiiii.*	miliaria lxiiii.	*cinquecen-sessanta quattro miglia.*
econd ention	*clxxxviii leguas.*	ciento treinta y ocho leguas.	ciento treinta y ocho leguas.	milliaria dxl.	miliaria dxl.	*cinquecen-sessanta quattro miglia.*

From this table it will be seen that the erroneous one hundred and thirty-eight leagues do not tally with the erroneous five hundred and forty miles; but the most striking fact that this table presents to our notice is that the *Dati poem* is the only one of these documents that has the number right in both places; and it might at first sight appear a very simple and easy thing for Dati to see that what was right measurement in the one case must be the right measurement in the other, even although the other copyists had failed to realise this fact. But not so. Dati composed his poem from the Latin translation, and if the edition from which he worked had been as faulty as that of Plannck, now under notice, he could have had no means of deciding which number was right, the dlxiiii of the first mention, or the dxl of the second. We have the means of knowing, but only because we possess the various copies of the Spanish, which state the distance in leagues. The necessary conclusion then is that Dati worked from a copy either MS. or printed, in which the number was right in both places; and this conclusion is corroborated by the fact that, of the Spanish documents, the Valencia MS. shows the number right in the first mention, and the Ambrosian text shows it right in the second. Furthermore, I observe that Dati, who distinctly states that his poem was 'tradocta di latino,' gives the letter the date of Feb. 15th, a date which occurs in the Spanish, but not in the Latin texts which we possess. It follows, therefore, that if he worked from a printed text, that edition is lost to us.

But there remains the alternative that he worked from the MS. Latin translation, and that the latter had been fully rendered from the original Spanish, but was afterwards modified by the compositor in setting it up in type. That such was in reality the case the reader will find proved beyond all dispute at the close of this disquisition. It therefore remains that, while there is no reason to suppose that an edition is lost, the edition by Planck, consisting of 4 leaves, with 33 lines to the page, must take the lead among those which are known to us.

But now we come to the very interesting subject of the original Spanish. Columbus's manuscript letter is lost, and the only representatives of it with which we are acquainted are the manuscript copies already mentioned at Simancas and Valencia, published respectively by Navarrete and Senhor de Varnhagen, and the valuable printed text in the Ambrosian Library, for the reproduction of which by photo-zincography all who are interested in the subject are so deeply indebted to the enlightened liberality of the Marquis d'Adda. The two former transcripts are confessedly made at a much later date, while to the latter bibliographers give the credit of the date of 1493. At the end of the Simancas copy is the expression : 'Esta carta envio Colon al Escribano de Racion de las islas halladas en las Indias e otra de sus altezas.' This office of Escribano de Racion was held by Luis de Santangel. The Valencia copy had no such sentence at the end, but simply bore the title: 'Carta del Almirante á D. Gabriel Sanches.' The Ambrosian text photozincographed by the Marquis d'Adda bore a similar expression at the end to that of the Simancas copy, but with a difference; thus: 'Esta carta embio Colon al Escrivano de Racion de las Islas halladas en las Indias. Contenida a otra de sus altezas.' Under these circumstances the Marquis d'Adda, accepting the pre-supposed fact that Columbus had addressed two similar letters to the two above-named officials, very naturally regarded the Ambrosian text as derived from the Simancas MS. A collation of the three texts, *inter se*, and with the Latin translation of Cosco, exhibits, however, the following results:—the Valencia MS. addressed to Gabriel Sanchez is almost a verbatim repetition of the Simancas text addressed to the Escribano de Racion, while the Ambrosian text also addressed to the Escribano de Racion agrees with the Latin text addressed to Gabriel Sanchez in certain forms of expression, which are entirely different from those used in common in the Valencia and Simancas MSS. to describe the same thing. This perplexing result has been stated by Senhor de Varnhagen in the little work published last year already referred to, and I can confirm it by actual careful collation of all the four documents. The *primâ facie* inference from this fact would, I think, be that the Escribano de Racion and Gabriel Sanchez, either really were, or by some mistake had been taken to be, identical.

A very high authority on such a subject, Señor de Gayangos, in the learned article already referred to, distinctly maintains the dispatch of two letters to the said two officials, whereas Senhor de Varnhagen not only limits the dispatch to one single address, but goes so far as to conclude that the Spanish printed text, from which he believes the Latin to be translated, is in fact the letter addressed to the sovereigns, with the change only of 'vuestras' into 'sus.' But as his Excellency has given much careful thought to this matter, and has, under the guidance of a most judicious criticism, supplied an amended text, derived from a collation of the different texts, it is but justice to him and to the subject itself to give a literal translation of his remarks. This is the more requisite as I shall have to submit some facts which seem to me to lead to conclusions differing from some of those arrived at by my learned friend.

His Excellency says: 'We hold it for certain that the said *primitive* edition (the Ambrosian) which we have had the opportunity of seeing in Milan, *must have given origin* to the text published in Rome the 25th April* of that same year (1493) by Cozco, who perhaps from not being able to transfer easily to the Latin the last part of it, cut it off. The said fact is principally *shown* by the mistake of the date of 14th (instead of 4th) of March, which could not be in the letter of Columbus, as he had left Lisbon before that day; nor would it be reasonable to suppose that the error would be repeated in the same manner, if said

* It should be 29th. The mistake is copied from Navarrete.

original had been kept in sight. Still less could the repetition of such a mistake be conceived, if the original manuscript were different.'

Now, before we proceed to an examination of this matter, the first thing requisite is to lay before the reader a specific difference which exists between the Spanish and the Latin texts. In the Spanish (I quote from the Ambrosian text) the letter closes thus: 'Esto segun el fecho asi en breve. Fecha en la calavera sobre las Yslas de Canaria a xv de Febrero mil et quatrocientos et noventa y tres años.'

Then comes a

'Nyma que venia dentro en la carta.'

'Despues desta escripto y estando en mar de Castilla salyo tanto viento conmigo sul y sueste que me ha fecho descargar la navios por cosi (correr?) aqui en este puerto de Lysbona oy, que fue la mayor maravilla del mundo. Adonde acordé escrivir a sus altezas. En todas las Yndias he siempre hallado los tenporales como en Mayo, adonde yo fuy en xxxiii dias et volvi en xxviii, salvo questas tormentas me han detenido xiiii dias corriendo por esta mar. Dizen aqua todos los honbres de la mar que jamas ovo tan mal yvierno no ni tantas perdidas de naves, fecha a xiiii dias de marco.

'Esta carta embio Colon al Escrivano de racion de las Islas halladas en las Indias. Contenida a otra de sus altezas;' which I translate thus:—

'After this letter was written, as I was in the sea of Castille, there arose a south-west wind, which compelled me to lighten my vessels and run this day into this port of Lisbon, an event which I consider the most marvellous thing in the world, and whence I resolved to write to their Highnesses. In all the Indies I have always found the weather like that in the month of May. I reached them in thirty-three days, and returned in twenty-eight, with the exception that these storms detained me fourteen days knocking about in this sea. All seamen say that they have never seen such a severe winter nor so many vessels lost.

'Done on the fourteenth day of March.'

This letter was sent by Columbus to the Chancellor of the Exchequer respecting the islands found in the Indies, enclosing another for their Highnesses'.

The Latin translation ends very differently; thus: 'Hæc ut gesta sunt sic breviter enarrata. Vale. Ulisbone, pridie Idus Martii.'

Now the reader will observe that in the above 'nyma,' or postscript, Columbus states that on the day of his reaching Lisbon he resolved to write to their Highnesses, and we know from his diaries that that day was the 4th of March, and yet at the end the postscript is dated the 14th of March, a day on which we know, from the said diaries, that he was off Cape St. Vincent on his way from Lisbon to Spain, which he was then on the point of reaching at the harbour of Palos.

The Latin, it will be perceived, repeats this discrepancy in a more distinct shape, by bringing the name of Lisbon immediately into connection with the 14th of March, of which the words: 'pridie Idus Martii' are the equivalent.

With these specialities in his mind, the reader will be able with greater clearness to follow the following disquisition :—

The perfectly sound piece of criticism by Senhor de Varnhagen which we have just read, is based upon the accepted premiss that it was on the 4th of March that Columbus dispatched to the King and Queen the letter describing his voyage, with the nema attached. The words of the 'nema' itself make such an inference highly reasonable. It states that 'el viento me ha fecho descargar los navios por correr aqui en este puerto da Lisbona *hoy* . . . adonde acordé de escribir a sus altezas.'—'The wind made me unload the ships to run into this port of Lisbon to-day . . . where I resolved to write to their Highnesses.' The diary shows that this day was the 4th of March, and hence, *primâ facie*, the date of '14th of March' in the nema would appear to be not written by Columbus, but a blunder of the printer of the Ambrosian text. This natural inference *appears* confirmed, I find, by the distinct statement of Ferdinand Columbus that on his father's arrival in Lisbon on the 4th—'Subito espedi un corriero a' Re Catolici con la nuova della sua venuta' —'he immediately dispatched a courier to the Catholic Sovereigns with the news of his arrival.'

Now, supposing, for I do not take it for granted, that this statement of Fernando's, written many years after, was correct, and that his father carried out his intention of writing to the Sovereigns from Lisbon, that statement does not tell us that he then *sent on the account of his voyage;* and if we inquire a little further, we have good reason to suppose that he did *not* forward it on that day.

There is no mention in his Diary of his so doing, although the act would be of sufficient importance to call for mention. He was in a country where his success in the cause of Spain was regarded with intense animosity. He was ignorant of the whereabouts of the Sovereigns, and in prospect of an early arrival in Spain, when he both would gain the necessary information, and could send on his precious missive in perfect safety. In harmony with these suggestions of mine, I find that Herrera, the historiographer, who had in his charge all the Columbian documents, states that on Wednesday, the 13th March, Columbus left Lisbon for Seville in his caravel. On Thursday, the 14th, before daybreak, he was off Cape St. Vincent. On Friday, the 15th, at mid-day, he entered the port of Palos, whence he had sailed on the 3rd of August of the previous year. *And having learned that the Catholic Sovereigns were at Barcelona*, he at first thought of going there in his caravel; but subsequently resolving not to go to Barcelona by sea, he *announced his arrival to the Catholic Sovereigns, and sent a summary of what had happened to him, reserving the more complete narrative for their immediate presence.* The *reply* reached him in Seville, and contained expressions of joy at his safe arrival and at the success of his voyage, offered him rewards and honours, and commanded him to make haste to go to Barcelona. Now, it will be remembered that Columbus' narrative was already written, and dated February 15th or 18th, and only waiting to be dispatched, and had attached to it the nema, which Mr. Gayangos tells us was a piece of paper placed on the outside of a letter like a padlock, and over which the seal was put. On this nema, beyond all question, was the date of March 4th; and if, as I gather from Herrera's statement, Columbus dispatched this narrative of his voyage, not from Lisbon on the 4th March, but from Palos on the 15th, or the 16th, it is not unlikely that on the 14th, when he was nearing the Spanish harbour from which he was looking forward to be able to dispatch it in safety, he should have altered the remote date of the 4th, which agreed with the wording of the nema at the time of writing it, into the later date of the 14th, which was more in accordance with the date of dispatch. We know that the letter to the Sovereigns was enclosed in the letter to the Escribano de Racion; and the sentence printed at the end of the Ambrosian text bears the aspect of an endorsement of the letter by that officer's secretary. The date of the Sovereigns' reply from Barcelona, March 30th, is in entire harmony, as regards lapse of time, with the dispatch of Columbus' letter from Palos on the 15th or 16th of the month. The Latin translation was completed on the 29th April, a full month after the arrival of the letter in Barcelona. There was plenty of time, therefore, it is true, for the letter to have been printed in Spanish, and for that Spanish to have served for the translation into Latin; but if my suggestion, as derived from the above data, be correct, that the alteration of 4 to 14 on the nema was made by Columbus himself, my friend Senhor de Varnhagen's conclusion that the Spanish printed text *must* have served for that translation becomes a *non sequitur*. Such alteration by Columbus would naturally lead to the erroneous 'ulisbone, pridie idus Martii' in the Latin text, without the intervention of the Spanish printed text, in which that alteration would of course also be copied.

I have stated these facts to show that the occurrence of March 14th, both in the Ambrosian text and the Latin translation, does not, as Senhor de Varnhagen concluded, prove of necessity that the latter was derived from the former, but from a common origin, to wit, in all probability the original MS. of Columbus. But now that I have shown that the Latin *need not* have been derived from the Ambrosian, I proceed to show that it *could not* have been so.

In the Ambrosian we find Guanahani spelt Guanaham; the island of Matinino called Matremonio, &c.; while in the

Latin text we find the first name correctly written Guanahani, Matinino is more nearly correctly written Mateunin; and we have the name of an island, Charis, which is left out in the Spanish altogether. But as the Latin translator possessed no special knowledge by which he could make such corrections, it is clear that the Ambrosian text could not have served as the basis for the Latin; whereas if the two were derived from a common source, the errors of the Ambrosian text would be those of its copyist, while the accurate rendering of the corresponding passages in the Latin would be the result, not of correction, as Senhor de Varnhagen suggests, but of attention to the original.

Upon this head Senhor de Varnhagen writes as follows:—

'The Latin texts contain a correction

of the words Guanahanin, Charis (Caribes or Caraibes), and Mateunin (Matinino); but these corrections, if perchance it should be proved that they were made at the time of the first edition, and not afterwards (which we cannot here examine, not having the different editions at hand), may have been pointed out by the editor himself in sight of the original after the publication of the printed text; or by Columbus himself, on receiving it on his road to Barcelona, in order that some correct copies might be sent to Rome, by way of communicating the news of the discovery that had been made, with the view of obtaining the famous Bull from Alexander VI.'

Now it is pretty clear that the Latin translation had nothing in the world to do with the Papal Bull. The name of *De* Cosco indicates that the translator was a Spaniard—and it is reasonable to assume that a Spaniard would be selected to translate from Spanish into Latin;—therefore we may fairly suppose that the translation was made in Spain. It was not completed till the 29th of April—'tertio kalendas maii'—(not the 25th, an error of Navarrete's, which Senhor de Varnhagen has adopted)—and the first bull was issued on the 3rd of May. The interval of four days is scarcely sufficient to allow of the formal dispatch of the document to Rome, its presentation and the drawing up of the bull, much less if it had to undergo revision by Columbus, still less if it be a question of correction of printed proofs set up in type at Rome in that short interval. It is tolerably evident, then, that the Latin was sent to Rome, not to the Pope, but only for printing. If, therefore, the missive to the Pope was in Spanish, and included this letter, the corrections by Columbus or by Sanchez, suggested by Senhor de Varnhagen, would have been far better applied to the Spanish than to the Latin, instead of the reverse, as suggested.

It should, however, be borne in mind that in those days proofs were not sent out for revision; but as a doubt may reasonably be entertained on this point, on the score of the many imaginable possibilities that may not have been foreseen or taken into consideration in this criticism, I will now proceed to demonstrate that the Spanish and the Latin printed texts certainly are derived from different, though similar, documents. That they should be similar is natural, the one being written by Columbus from the other, with such trivial changes as may have dropped from his pen in transcribing.

First: we have a Spanish text, the endorsement of which shows it to have been sent to the Escribano de Racion. That this officer was Luis de Santangel we know for certainty from Argensola's *Anales de Aragon*, lib. i. cap. 10, p. 99, *et seq.*, where he tells us that when the King looked coldly on Columbus' proposals, because the royal finances had been drained by war, Isabella offered her jewels for the enterprise; but this was rendered needless, as 'Luis de Santangel, Escrivano de Racion de Aragon, advanced seventeen thousand florins for the expenses of the Armada.' This leaves no room for doubt that Columbus should immediately send a copy of his letter to Santangel. In it was enclosed the copy addressed to the Sovereigns.* This text sent to Santangel consisted of a letter dated February 15th, and a postscript, announcing the arrival off Lisbon on the 4th, subsequently altered to the 14th March.

Secondly: we have a Latin text, distinctly stated to have been translated from a letter addressed to the Royal Treasurer, Gabriel Sanchez. We have

* In pursuance of his idea that not two, but only one letter, was despatched to head-quarters, Senhor de Varnhagen has translated the words of the endorsement, 'Contenida a otra de Sus Altezas,' 'Contenida *en* otra,' &c.; and then, reasoning from the impossibility of Columbus showing such familiarity with the Sovereigns, argues, that the letter was in fact addressed to them only. With all respect I submit that the natural rendering is 'Contenida la otra de Sus Altezas;' *Angl.* 'Contained the other of their Highnesses;' or, as it would be clearer in French, 'Y contenue l'autre de Leurs Altesses:' and Santangel appropriately appears as bearer of the missive to the Sovereigns.

thus clearly two letters addressed to two persons, but to annihilate this duality Senhor de Varnhagen suggests 'Why not suppose that this last name, Gabriel Sanxis, which Cosco thought it necessary to announce, was the result of his own verifications? He would inquire in Rome of the Catholic delegates the name of the Escribano de Racion, and they would give him that of the Treasurer General.' But this is inventing *one surmise* to fortify *another*, whereas Senhor de Varnhagen's own zealous research had provided evidence to prove a contrary *fact*. The Marquis d'Adda has kindly sent me a photo-lithograph of a fragment of an Italian version of this letter, of which His Excellency Senhor de Varnhagen had found the title in the catalogue of the Ambrosian Library. This fragment distinctly states it to have been a copy of one 'sent by the Grand Treasurer to his brother, Joane Sanxis.'

Thus, beyond all question, it is proved that Columbus addressed these two several letters to these two different persons, from one of which the Spanish text was printed, and from the other the Latin translation was made and subsequently printed. And having reached this point, we see clearly that my suggestion of Columbus having altered the date of 4th March to 14th *must* have been correct; and furthermore, that he copied the date of '14th' on whichever of these two letters was written last, because, while it stands March 14th *in totidem verbis* in one, it is rendered 'pridie idus Martii' (which means the same thing) in the translation from the other. We see in this date 'Ulisbone, pridie idus Martii,' a proof that the copy from which the Latin was made, consisted, like the original of the Ambrosian Spanish text, of a complete letter with the 'nema' added, because the place Lisbon is derived from the language at the beginning of the nema, and the date from Columbus' alteration at the end. Although the printer, Plannck, inserted nothing of the 'nema' beyond the said place and date, which he placed at the end of the body of the letter in lieu of February 15th, we have a clear proof that De Cosco had really translated the letter and nema as they stand in the Spanish, for when we come to look into Dati's poem, which he distinctly states to be translated from the Latin, we find *the date of February 15th retained, but no allusion to the contents of the nema, which, being detached, had evi-*

dently not reached his hands. This fact, and others observable in his text, especially when examined in combination with the Italian, which also came from the Sanchez original, show that Dati worked from Cosco's manuscript translation. As to whether of the two printed texts, the Ambrosian Spanish or Planck's Latin, can claim priority, we have no present means of deciding, but that the preference is due to the Spanish under critical correction is manifest, since it has been exposed to modifications from a compositor only, while the Latin has passed through the two ordeals of a translation and a compositor's alterations. For this reason I adopted the Spanish in the text of the second edition of the Letters, with the remark that it replaced the very worst Latin text which I could have adopted.

viz. that taken by Navarrete from the *España Illustrada.* The faults in the Ambrosian text are many and great, and this has led Señor de Gayangos to suggest that it was printed, not in Spain, but in Portugal, probably Lisbon. An opinion from one so eminent has great weight, but while yielding to none in sincere respect for the judgment of my distinguished friend, I confess I think that the circumstances of the letter point, as Senhor de Varnhagen has stated, to Barcelona for the place of printing. Mr. Winter Jones, the Principal Librarian of the British Museum, and late Keeper of the Department of Printed Books, whose bibliographical knowledge is so well known, tells me that he recollects having seen the initial letter S, which commences the Ambrosian text, but, in spite of great research, I have failed to find it or the corresponding type in any work in our vast library. It is here well to remark that no kind of *fac-simile* is so baulking to bibliographic comparison as the photographic. The respective sizes of the letters are altered, and the outline is rendered broken and rotten. A *fac-simile* of this same letter, done by the hand, was published in Milan in 1863, in the sixteenth volume of the *Biblioteca Rara* of G. Daelli, and gives the type a far firmer appearance than that in the photograph. It is obvious that an opportunity is afforded of correcting the mistakes in the Ambrosian text from the other texts which we possess. This has been done with great skill and judgment by Senhor de Varnhagen by collation with the Simancas, the Valencia, and the Latin texts; to these aids I have added the Italian poem of Giuliano

Dati, and the Italian fragment, for which I have been indebted to the kindness of the Marquis d'Adda.

I must not close this bibliographical notice without tendering my warmest thanks to my friends, William Brenchley Rye, Esq., the learned Keeper of the Printed Books in the British Museum; and Robert Edmund Graves, Esq., one of the most accomplished of his Assistant-Librarians;—to the former for most kindly making out the foregoing list of incunabula of the first letter, and the latter for very valuable help in my search for collateral texts by which to fortify my conclusions in the toilsome examination which I have here brought to a termination.

LONDON:
Printed by JOHN STRANGEWAYS, Castle St. Leicester Sq.

www.ingramcontent.com/pod-product-compliance
Lightning Source LLC
Chambersburg PA
CBHW022153020726
47496CB00008B/2695
* 9 7 8 3 7 4 4 7 2 7 8 4 6 *